Published by Two Lions, New York

www.apub.com

Amazon, the Amazon logo, and Two Lions are trademarks
of Amazon.com, Inc., or its affiliates.

two lions

ISBN-13: 9781477847763 (hardcover)
ISBN-10: 1477847766 (hardcover)
ISBN-13: 9781477897768 (eBook)
ISBN-10: 1477897763 (eBook)

The illustrations were rendered digitally.
Book design by Jeff Mack and Vera Soki
Editor: Margery Cuyler

Printed in China
First edition
10 9 8 7 6 5 4 3 2 1

For my good friend, David Hyde Costello

DUCK IN THE FRIDGE

written and illustrated by
JEFF MACK

OK, KIDDO. IT'S TIME FOR BED.

two lions

...IT ALL STARTED WHEN I FOUND A DUCK IN THE FRIDGE.
A DUCK IN THE FRIDGE?!
MOTHER

That's right. One night,
when I was a kid, I found
a duck in the fridge.

What a mess! When I
went to get a towel . . .

I tried to get ready for bed,
but the ducks were everywhere.
I couldn't brush my teeth.

I couldn't put on my pj's.

And, worst of all, I couldn't sleep!

I gave the ducks some crackers,
but they ate them all.
Then they ordered out for pizza.

WHO'S GOING TO PAY FOR ALL OF THIS?

So I called 1-800-DUCK-B-GONE.
They sent me a special kit
to scare away the ducks.

The sheep just sat there watching TV.
The ducks were not afraid.

BUY MORE PIZZA! BUY MORE PIZZA!

MOTHER GOOSE

So I ordered a bigger, better, scarier kit.

That didn't work either.
The dogs stayed up
all night playing cards.

Meanwhile, the ducks
and the sheep started
their own band.

There was only
one thing left to do.

Well, those cows didn't scare anyone,
but they did throw a wild party.
How would I ever get to sleep now?

That's when I saw the light.

Maybe I didn't need to
scare them away after all.

I opened the book and started to read.

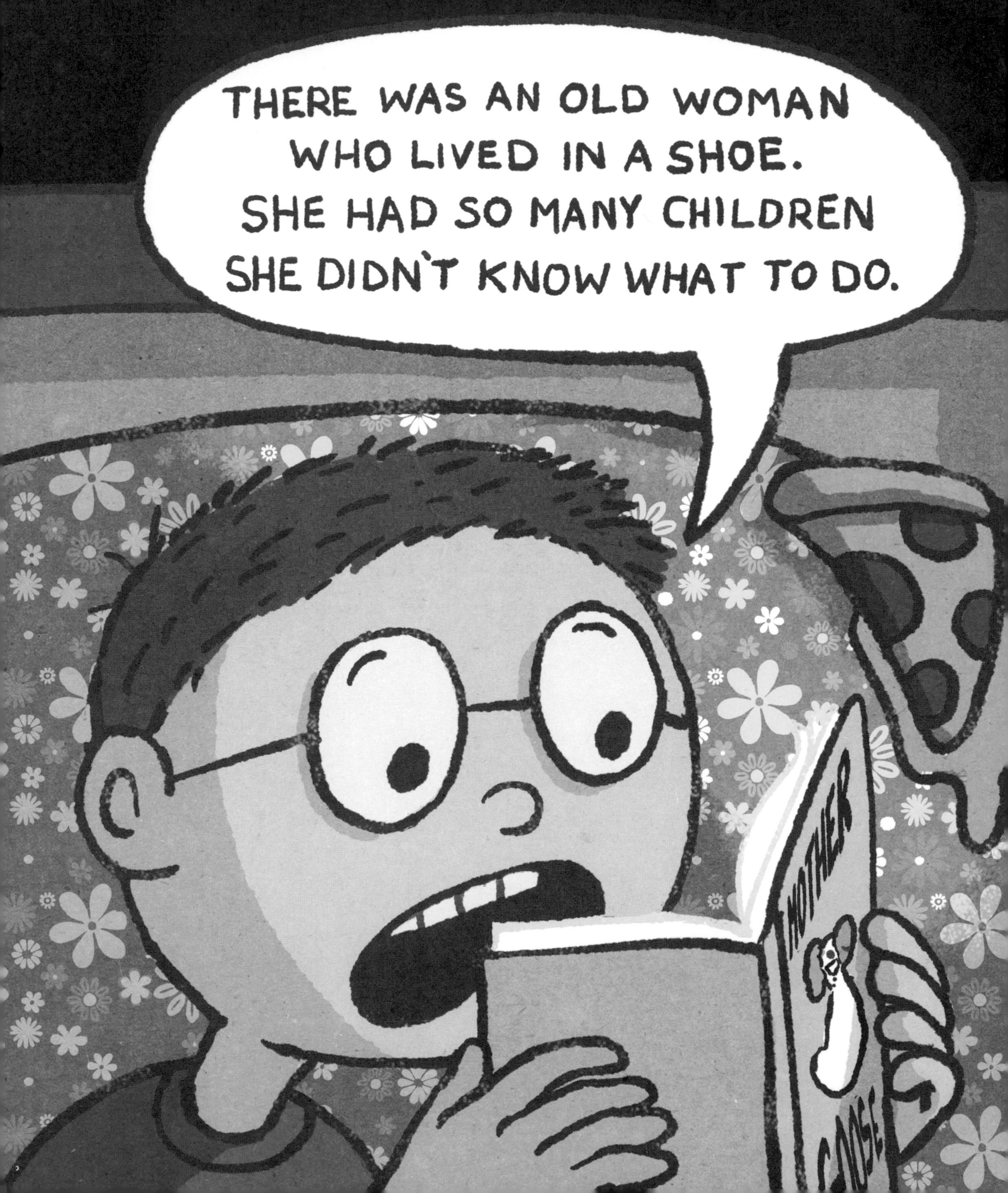

They seemed curious,
so I read more.

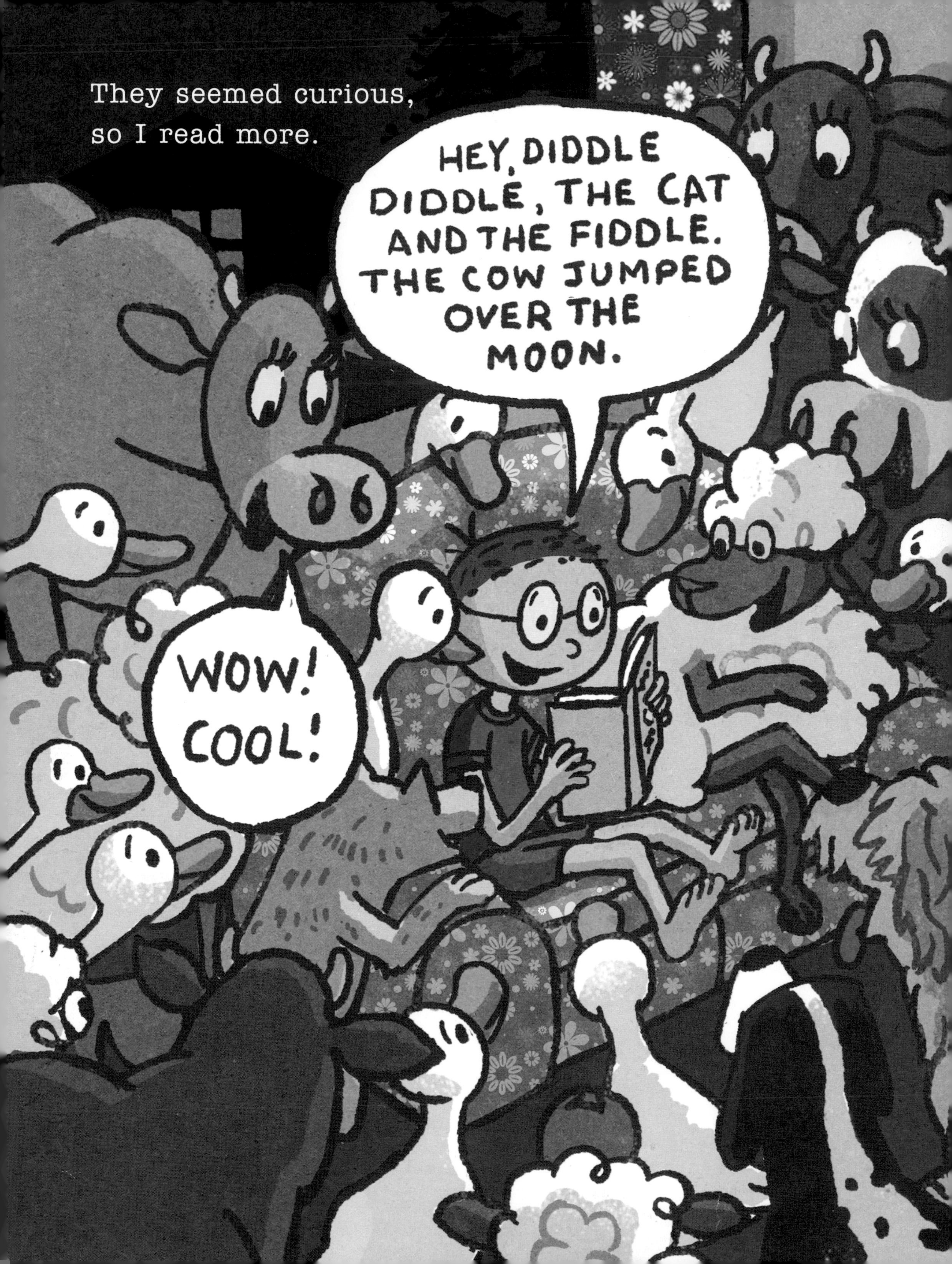

They liked it! They really liked it!

I said, "If everyone goes to sleep
right now, I promise I'll read
more tomorrow night."
And guess what?

They all went to sleep.
Just like that.

The next night, I read
the book again, and
the same thing happened.
Not only was it fun to read,
but we all got plenty of sleep.

SO THAT'S WHY I READ MOTHER GOOSE TO YOU EVERY NIGHT.
GOOD NIGHT, KIDDO.
GOOD NIGHT, DADDY.